SHUTTLE BURN
Roy Bentley

ANDRE DEUTSCH

First published 1984 by
André Deutsch Limited
105 Great Russell Street London WC1

Colour separations by
Dot Gradations Ltd, Chelmsford, Essex

Typeset by Diagraphic Typesetters Ltd

Printed in Hong Kong

ISBN 0 233 97624 8

On the edge of space, three hundred kilometres up, shuttle G36 circled the earth in low orbit. Inside sat four young 'spacers', nervous and tense but ready for their first re-entry without an instructor.

Nearby in Space-station B19 a flight controller finished his final checks.
"B19 to G36 – you are GO for re-entry," he radioed, "Good luck and happy landings."

"Watch out, Earth, here we come," called out Tycho at the radar controls.
"Watch out us, here comes Earth," corrected Gemma.
"Think of all the dangers we might…"

"That's right," interrupted Ross their pilot. "We could run into some bumpy weather down there, not like the smooth emptiness of space."
"But it's home," added Cassi, "and it's time to go! Retro-burn minus twenty seconds; final systems check now!"

"All warning lights green," the others reported in turn. Seven, six, pumps on, fuel on, three, two, one, fire!

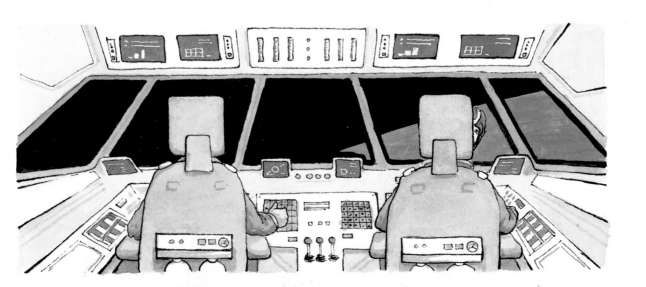

For three minutes the retro-rockets blazed, slowing them down and using up all their fuel. At the end of the burn the shuttle would be no more than a huge ninety tonne glider.

Their speed, their direction had to be right. Their flight path curved half way round the Earth aiming for a runway only metres wide. As Gemma had once said, it was like throwing a pea into an eggcup – from five kilometres, first time!

"Engines off," Cassi radioed. "G36 out of orbit. Goodbye B19, goodbye space, over and out."

They were falling, speeding towards the earth's thick atmosphere and the blazing heat of re-entry.
Ross fired the steering thrusters, turning the shuttle so the thickest heat resisting tiles would protect them from the very highest temperatures.

Quietly they watched the wings through the windows. A faint glow lit the front edges, they were entering the outer fringes of the atmosphere, and the most dangerous part of their mission.

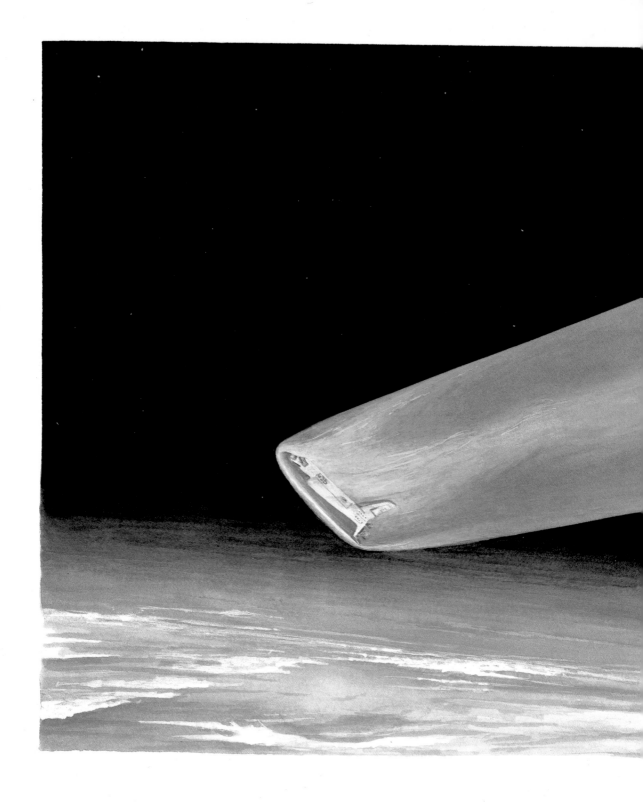

Down they plunged, the glow brightening, spreading ....
The shuttle was encased in a blazing flaming cloud – the
fire-ball.

Cut off by the intense heat from radio contact the four cadets were locked inside, utterly alone.

Suddenly a red warning light switched on.
"Red Alert, system two," called out Ross in alarm.

Gemma checked on the central computer, "Saturn! There's a
massive overheat on the left wing. WE'VE LOST A TILE!"

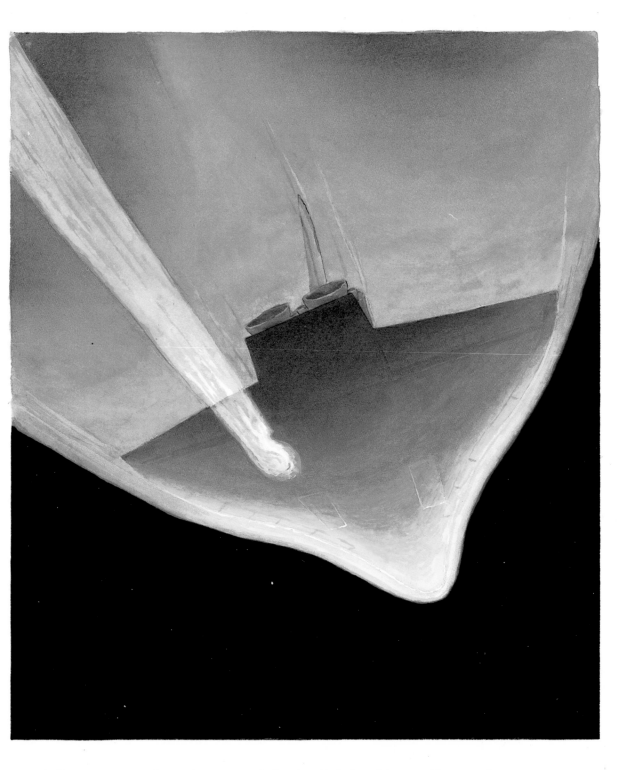

There were six minutes of fireball left. Six endless minutes
whilst the raging heat roared through one small chink in the
shuttle's armour. Eating deeper and deeper into the wing it
was burning, melting away metal, wires, pipes – everything!

Braked by the air the shuttle slowed and the fire-ball dimmed. They were through!

"Red Alert, Red Alert," called Cassi, "G36 damaged on re-entry."

The reply from ground control came at once, "OK, G36, we are preparing for an emergency landing – report damage, over."

At the computer Gemma worked frantically, there were red lights everywhere!

Finally she looked round. "Most of the left wing circuits are dead or damaged, but the wing itself seems OK."

Loudspeakers rang out across the landing field, calling the emergency crews to action.

Fire engines, ambulances, rescue vehicles of all kinds raced towards the main runway.

Two supersonic jets roared off, heading for the damaged
space-craft.

Thankfully the cadets watched the jets flash past, turn and pull in alongside.

Slowly, carefully the lead plane slid sideways and down, right under the shuttle's damaged left wing.

"There's a smoking, burning hole," reported the pilot, "just behind the main left landing wheel."

Ross wrestled grimly with the half dead controls swinging the massive 'glider' from side to side to lose speed and height. He had only five minutes left to slow down. If they overshot the airfield there was no going back, no second chance.

Finally, with an endless, sliding, banking turn he did it –
they were down to landing speed and there was the main
runway dead ahead!

"Lower the wheels," commanded ground control.

Cassi reached over and pushed the three levers forward.
"Two green lights," she reported, "the right and front wheels
are down and locked – looks like the left one is dead."

"No it's not!" one of the jet pilots called out, "the left one is down too."
"But we don't know if it's locked," replied ground control, "it could just fold up on landing."

"Prepare for crash landing," ground control instructed. The fire crews switched on their pumps sending huge fountains of foam over the runway, covering it in a thick white carpet.

Faster and faster they pumped, anxiously watching the shuttle speeding towards them. If the left wheel did fold up on landing the foam would soften the crash, help the damaged shuttle to slide, and with luck put out any sparks and fires.

Lowering the enormous space-plane, Ross banked
it over, searching for the hard concrete runway
with the wheel he *knew* was down and locked.

There was a crashing jolt and an awful tearing
squeal. Gripping the controls, Ross nursed the
juddering shuttle as it skated along on one wheel,
kicking up plumes of foam.
"One down," he muttered, "one to go."

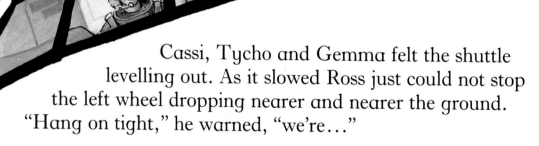

Cassi, Tycho and Gemma felt the shuttle
levelling out. As it slowed Ross just could not stop
the left wheel dropping nearer and nearer the ground.
"Hang on tight," he warned, "we're…"

Bang! The shuttle twisted and lurched as the left wheel ploughed into the thick foam, thumped onto the runway, and held!

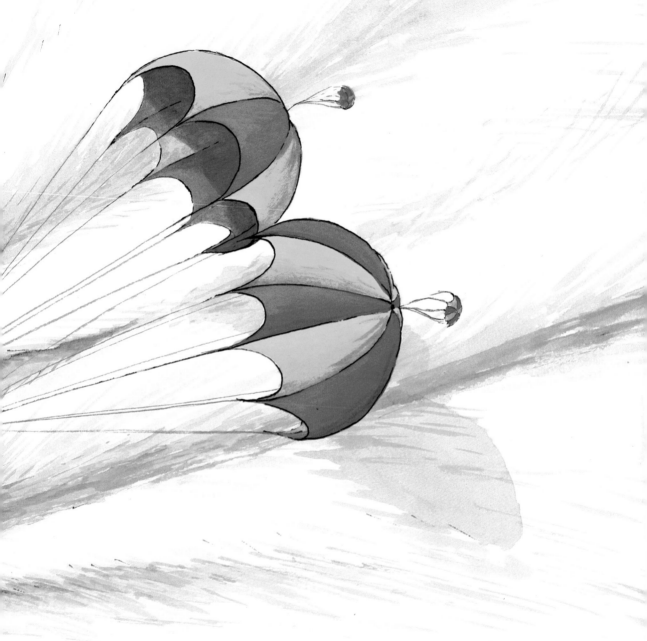

Cassi opened the airbrakes and the emergency parachutes, fearing at any moment that the wheel would fold.

Finally the huge shuttle slithered to a stop, and safety.

Swiftly the cadets switched off all flight systems and made the shuttle safe to leave. Gemma opened the outer hatch and they looked out to find themselves in a sea of foam, surrounded by splattered emergency vehicles and crew.

Tycho grinned,
"Not a crash landing but a splash landing I'd say!"

FLIGHT PATH

Retro-burn

turnround

ready for re-entry

fireball starts

tile lost

final approach

landing